SPANYOL, Jessica

Carlo and the really nice
librarian

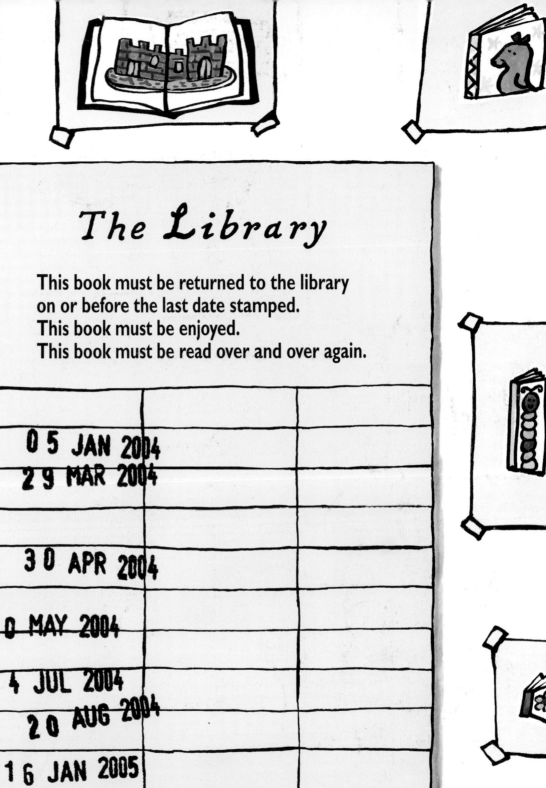

The Library

This book must be returned to the library
on or before the last date stamped.
This book must be enjoyed.
This book must be read over and over again.

0 5 JAN 2004		
2 9 MAR 2004		
3 0 APR 2004		
1 0 MAY 2004		
1 4 JUL 2004		
2 0 AUG 2004		
1 6 JAN 2005		

First published 2004 by Walker Books Ltd
87 Vauxhall Walk, London SE11 5HJ

2 4 6 8 10 9 7 5 3 1

© 2004 Jessica Spanyol

The right of Jessica Spanyol to be identified as author/illustrator of this work
has been asserted by her in accordance
with the Copyright, Designs and Patents Act 1988

This book has been typeset in Spanyol Bold

Printed in China

British Library Cataloguing in Publication Data:
a catalogue record for this book is available from the British Library

ISBN 0-7445-9689-0 (hb)
ISBN 1-84428-512-X (pb)

www.walkerbooks.co.uk

Carlo
and the Really Nice
Librarian

WALKER BOOKS
AND SUBSIDIARIES
LONDON · BOSTON · SYDNEY · AUCKLAND

Jessica Spanyol

One day Dad took Carlo and Crackers to the new library.

The Library

Fiction

Children's Books →

Welcome

"Wow!" said Carlo when he saw all the books.

Dad called after Carlo, "I'm going to be just around this corner if you need me."

The library was very impressive.
There were colourful posters.
There were chairs
with wheels on.

And there was the longest desk Carlo had ever seen. "Come on, Crackers," said Carlo.

"Wheee!"

"Hello, I'm **Mrs Chinca**.
What's your name?"
"Carlo," whispered Carlo.
"And who is this?"
asked **Mrs Chinca**.

"That's Crackers. He's my cat."
Mrs Chinca the librarian
seemed a bit scary.

"What sort of books do you like, Carlo?" asked **Mrs Chinca**.

"All sorts," Carlo said quietly.

"Very good. Well, let me tell you about our library books. Come on, Carlo,

follow me."

"This is a lovely bedtime story," said Mrs Chinca.

"Just look at these beautiful pictures, Carlo."

"And this is a very exciting read."

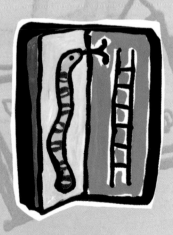

Carlo couldn't believe
how much **Mrs Chinca**
knew about books.

"This is one of my favourites,"
said **Mrs Chinca** in a muffled voice.
"Oh, I've got that one at home!"
Carlo said excitedly.

Carlo was beginning to think that
Mrs Chinca wasn't as scary as
he had first thought. She was being
such a good and helpful librarian.

"Would you like to read
a book with me?"
Mrs Chinca asked Carlo.
Carlo thought that would
be really good fun.

"*Brmm brmm,*" he said
when he saw the cars.
"*Tick tock,*" he said when he
saw the clock.

"ROAR!"

said **Mrs Chinca**
when she saw
the lion.

Carlo laughed
so much he got
his tail into
a tangle!

Next, **Mrs Chinca** asked Carlo to help her with her work. "You have such a lovely long neck, Carlo. Could you put these books on the top shelf?" Carlo really liked helping **Mrs Chinca**.

Then **Mrs Chinca** gave Carlo
his very own library card.

"Thank you so much!"
exclaimed Carlo.

Mrs Chinca's
purse

pencil
sharpener

keys

index cards

APPLICATION
The Library
NAME: Carlo
ADDRESS: 4 Valentine Road

library card

Mrs Chinca's pens
and pencils

rubber stamp

After Carlo had finished choosing his books,
Dad said it was time to go home.
Carlo felt sad to leave.
He couldn't believe he had ever been
scared of *Mrs Chinca*.

Mrs Chinca used Carlo's new library card
to check out all his books.
"Bye bye, Carlo. Bye bye, Crackers.
See you again soon," she said.
"Bye bye, Mrs Chinca," said Carlo.

Books Out
- The Garden
- Baby Owls
- Tweet Tweet
- Hello Robots
- Isabella Pig
- Shapes
- Trevor The Spider

As soon as Carlo got home, he showed Mum his library books and told her all about *Mrs Chinca*. "She's really nice and such good fun," said Carlo. "She sounds lovely, darling," said Mum.

It wasn't until Carlo opened his last book that he noticed something strange...

There was a tiny
bite-sized bit missing!

"Mrs Chinca really does love her books,"
laughed Carlo.

WALKER BOOKS is the world's leading
independent publisher of children's books.
Working with the best authors and illustrators
we create books for all ages, from babies
to teenagers – books your child will
grow up with and always remember. So…

FOR THE BEST CHILDREN'S BOOKS,
LOOK FOR THE BEAR